SKY, YOUR BREXIT!

La méthode post-Brexit
pour apprendre l'anglais

ISBN : 978-2-412-06009-4
Dépôt légal : septembre 2020
Imprimé en France par Normandie Roto Impression s.a.s. (2003177)

Correction : Muriel Mekies et Niamh O'Brien
Mise en page : Emilie Guillemin

Éditions First, un département d'Édi8
92, avenue de France
75013 Paris
Tél. 01 44 16 09 00 / Fax 01 44 16 09 01
Courriel : firstinfo@efirst.com / Internet : www.lisez.com

Jean-Loup Chiflet
avec Christiane Courbey

SKY, YOUR BREXIT!

La méthode post-Brexit
pour apprendre l'anglais

FIRST
ÉDITIONS

SOMMAIRE

FUCK THE BREXIT!

Alors ça y est ! Des mois qu'on nous bassine (en anglais « *to warm* » mais dans le cas présent « *to give us a pain in the neck* ») avec ce Brexit *at the bite-me-the-knot*, à la mords-moi le nœud (en anglais : « *dodgy* ») et voilà que nous devons accepter la triste vérité : le Brexit est là et il va falloir faire avec.

Triste vérité, dis-je, car personne ne semble mesurer, à l'heure où j'écris ces lignes, l'ampleur de cette catastrophe planétaire et surtout franco-britannique, si tant est que ce mot composé ait encore aujourd'hui une quelconque signification… Souvenez-vous, c'était vous, c'était moi, c'était nous, nos enfants et petits-enfants qui depuis les années 1960 adorions passer des vacances soi-disant studieuses chez Mr et Mrs Smith qui essayaient désespérément de nous convaincre que notre « *taylor* était riche » alors que nous ne pensions qu'à découvrir le plaisir des premiers baisers avec les petites Anglaises, sur fond de *Yellow Submarine*.

Elles s'appelaient Jane, Kate, Jenny, toutes aussi rousses et rougissantes sous le choc de nos lèvres encore ruisselantes des délicieux *eggs and bacon* de Mrs Smith. (Pour les jeunes Françaises, je précise que la réciprocité fonctionnait aussi bien, et je tiens à remercier Bobby qui a si gentiment déniaisé ma sœur).

En fait, nous étions bien naïfs, car nous aurions dû nous méfier de la si bien nommée « perfide Albion » : n'oublions pas qu'elle n'a cessé de nous humilier depuis Jeanne d'Arc, Waterloo, Trafalgar et, *last but not least*, qu'elle continue avec le Brexit ! Car maintenant, et je pèse mes mots, les Anglais sont en train de nous démontrer qu'ils ont atteint le comble de la turpitude sous la houlette de ce personnage maléfique, Boris Johnson, alias BoJo (le clown ?), à côté de qui l'évêque Cauchon ferait l'effet d'un piètre séminariste… Voilà pourquoi je vous invite solennellement à ne pas vous laisser mortifier une fois de plus, car l'heure est grave. Depuis des mois, BoJo souffle le chaud et le froid sur une Europe qui n'en peut plus d'être roulée dans la farine.

En tant qu'Européens responsables, faisons en sorte, nous les Français, d'être les premiers à réagir : utilisons notre arme favorite, l'humour, cette bonne vieille tradition française qui consiste à tremper notre plume dans le vitriol à l'image de nos courageux auteurs de libelles du Moyen Âge pour dénoncer la bêtise et l'injustice.

C'est ainsi qu'en accord avec les plus hautes autorités universitaires nous proposons notre propre version hautement pédagogique de la langue anglaise.

Non, le BoJoisme ne passera pas !

John-Wolf Whistle

LE BREXIT EN 200 PHRASES

MODE D'EMPLOI

Expression française destinée à faire passer un message important.

Vous ne pouvez pas avoir le beurre et l'argent du beurre.

Traduction en vigueur avant le Brexit (en anglais correct), mais désormais interdite.

You can't have your cake and eat it.

You can't have the butter and the money of the butter.

Nouvelle traduction (littérale et incorrecte), imposée par le Brexit.

BOSRIS

Boris, arrête de pratiquer
la langue de bois !

Stop that double talk, Boris!

↳ **Boris, stop to practise the tongue of wood!**

Ton Brexit, on va pas en faire tout un plat !

We won't kick up a fuss about your Brexit!

↳ **Your Brexit, we are not going to make all a dish!**

◆ ◆ ◆

Il faut arrêter d'enculer les mouches !

Stop splitting hairs!

↳ **Stop to sodomize flies!**

Arrête de jouer double jeu !

Stop double-dealing!

↳ **Stop to play double game!**

Arrête de passer de la brosse à reluire à la reine !

Stop flattering the Queen, will you?

↳ **Stop to pass the shine brush at the Queen!**

◆ ◆ ◆

Johnson, tu n'es pas sorti de l'auberge !

Johnson, you're not out of the woods yet!

↳ **Johnson, you are not out of the inn!**

Tu peux numéroter tes abattis !

You're in big trouble, Boris!

↳ **You can number your giblets!**

◆ ◆ ◆

Attention, on va te clouer le bec !

Careful, we're going to shut you up!

↳ **Careful, we're going to nail down your beak!**

Mêle-toi de tes oignons !

Stick to your knitting!

↳ **Mind your onions!**

◆ ◆ ◆

C'est un deal vraiment louche.

It's quite a dodgy deal.

↳ **It's a deal really squint.**

Boris, ta monnaie de singe,
on n'en veut pas.

Boris, we don't want any
of your Monopoly money.

↳ **Boris, your money of monkey,
we don't want it.**

Boris, arrête de faire l'andouille !

Boris, stop acting the fool!

↳ **Boris, stop to make the sausage!**

◆ ◆ ◆

Il te manque une case !

You've got a screw loose!

↳ **It misses you a box!**

Arrête, s'il te plaît, de faire des cacas nerveux !

Calm down, Boris!

↳ **Stop to make nervous poops, please!**

◆ ◆ ◆

Tu manges à tous les râteliers. C'est bien toi.

You seem to have a finger in every pie. That's just like you.

↳ **You eat at all racks. That's well you.**

Nous n'avons pas élevé les cochons ensemble !

You have a nerve to take liberties like that!

↳ **We have not raised pigs together!**

◆ ◆ ◆

Tu te fiches de nous comme de ta première chemise !

You don't give a damn about us!

↳ **You don't care about us like about your first shirt!**

Tu crois qu'on les a à zéro ?

Do you really think we're scared stiff?

↳ **You think we have them at zero?**

Tu veux nous en mettre plein la vue.

You want to blow us away.

↳ **You want to put us full the sight.**

◆ ◆ ◆

Tu voudrais même qu'on te refile la tour Eiffel…

You would even like to pinch the Eiffel Tower from us...

↳ **You would even like that we spin you the Tower Eiffel…**

Nous ne serons pas tes têtes de Turc.

We won't be your punchbag.

↳ **We won't be your heads of Turk.**

◆ ◆ ◆

Boris, le Port-Salut, pour toi, c'est fini.

No more Normandy cheese for you, Boris.

↳ **Boris, the Harbor-Hello, for you, it's finished.**

Du camembert ? Tu peux te brosser !

Camembert? You can whistle for it!

↳ **Camembert? You can brush you!**

◆ ◆ ◆

BoJo, ne ramène pas ta fraise en France.

BoJo, you'd better not show your face in France.

↳ **BoJo, don't bring back your strawberry in France.**

Tu dis que tu aimes la France ?
C'est du pipeau !

You say you love France?
What a load of crap!

↳ **You say you love France!**
It's pipe!

Ça va être ta fête !

You've got it coming to you!

↳ **It's going to be your party!**

◆ ◆ ◆

Si un jour tu viens à Paris,
tu as intérêt à raser les murs.

If you come to Paris one day,
you'd better keep a low profile.

↳ **If you come to Paris one day,
you'd better shave the walls.**

Il va falloir remettre les pendules à l'heure !

It's time to set things straight!

↳ **It's time to put the clocks at the hour!**

Il serait temps de faire amende honorable.

It's time for you to eat humble pie.

↳ **It would be time to make honorable almond.**

TALKING ABOUT HIM

Alors, qui c'est, le faux jeton ?

Tell me, who's the sneak?

↳ **So, who's the false token?**

Il ne serait pas un peu soupe au lait ?

I'm sure he has a short fuse.

↳ **Wouldn't he be a little soup at the milk?**

◆ ◆ ◆

Il prend la mouche à tout bout de champ.

He's quick to take offense.

↳ **He takes the fly at all ends of field.**

Qui c'est, le chouchou de la reine ?

Who is the Queen's pet?

↳ **Who is the cabbage-cabbage of the Queen?**

◆ ◆ ◆

BoJo fait de la lèche à la reine.

BoJo is good at groveling before the Queen.

↳ **BoJo makes licking at the Queen.**

C'est qui, le dindon de la farce ?

Who is the butt of the joke?

↳ **Who is the turkey of the stuffing?**

◆ ◆ ◆

BoJo a le ticket avec Donald.

BoJo has a thing for Donald.

↳ **BoJo has the ticket with Donald.**

BoJo et Donald ? C'est bonnet blanc et blanc bonnet.

BoJo and Donald? It's six of one and half a dozen of the other.

↳ **BoJo and Donald?**
It's white cap and cap white.

Ils s'entendent comme larrons en foire.

They are as thick as thieves.

↳ **They hear themselves like robbers in fair.**

◆ ◆ ◆

BoJo n'en a rien à secouer de l'Irlande.

BoJo doesn't give a damn about Ireland.

↳ **BoJo has nothing to shake of Ireland.**

BoJo est un ours mal léché.

BoJo is a gruff fellow.

↳ **BoJo is a bad licked bear.**

◆ ◆ ◆

C'est un chaud lapin.

He's a randy devil.

↳ **It's a hot rabbit.**

Il ne pense qu'à ça.

He has a dirty mind.

↳ **He only thinks of that.**

◆ ◆ ◆

BoJo aime beaucoup
les Marie-couche-toi-là.

BoJo loves easy women.

↳ **BoJo likes very much
the Mary-sleep-here.**

Boris a fait les 400 coups à Eton.

Boris often went out on the town at Eton.

↳ **Boris has made the 400 blows at Eton.**

Il est plein aux as.

He's rolling in it.

↳ **He's full to the aces.**

◆ ◆ ◆

Il a toujours un coup dans l'aile.

He's always had one too many.

↳ **He's always got a blow in the wing.**

BoJo me court sur le haricot.

BoJo is definitely getting
on my nerves.

↳ **BoJo runs me on the bean.**

◆ ◆ ◆

BoJo passe toujours
du coq à l'âne.

BoJo is always going off
on a tangent.

↳ **BoJo always passes
from the cock to the donkey.**

Il n'est pas franc du collier.

He's a fishy guy.

↳ **He isn't frank of the collar.**

◆ ◆ ◆

Il a un caractère de cochon.

He's got a foul temper.

↳ **He has a character of pig.**

C'est un casse-pieds.

He's a pain in the neck.

↳ **It's a break-feet.**

Il ne touche pas sa bille.

He's useless.

↳ **He doesn't touch his marble.**

◆ ◆ ◆

Il parle français comme
une vache espagnole.

He speaks broken French.

↳ **He speaks French like
a Spanish cow.**

Quand il parle français,
c'est du chinois pour nous.

When he speaks French,
it's all Greek to us.

↳ **When he speaks French,
it's Chinese for us.**

◆ ◆ ◆

Le Boris, il en a une sacrée couche.

Boris is as thick as two short planks.

↳ **The Boris, he has a sacred layer.**

Entre nous, BoJo n'a pas inventé l'eau tiède.

Between you and me, BoJo doesn't set the Thames on fire.

↳ **Between us, BoJo hasn't invented lukewarm water.**

◆ ◆ ◆

Boris aime amuser la galerie.

Boris loves to keep the crowd entertained.

↳ **Boris loves to amuse the gallery.**

Michel Barnier pense que BoJo est timbré.

Michel Barnier thinks that BoJo is crazy.

↳ **Michel Barnier thinks BoJo is stamped.**

Macron ne peut pas le sentir.

Macron can't stand him.

↳ **Macron can't smell him.**

◆ ◆ ◆

Johnson pense qu'il a le monde entier à sa botte.

Johnson thinks he has the whole world under his thumb.

↳ **Johnson thinks he has all the world at his boot.**

Boris balance toujours des vannes.

Boris is always making wisecracks.

↳ **Boris always swings sluices.**

◆ ◆ ◆

Ce type ferait passer un chameau par le chas d'une aiguille !

That guy could thread a camel through the eye of a needle!

↳ **That guy would make a camel pass through the eye of a needle!**

Quand je regarde la tête de BoJo, je me bidonne.

Whenever I look at BoJo's face, I just can't help laughing.

↳ **When I look at BoJo's head, I jerrican myself.**

◆ ◆ ◆

La coiffure de BoJo ? Pas piquée des hannetons !

BoJo's haircut? It's quite something!

↳ **BoJo's hair? Not picked of the June beetles!**

En plus, il a des pellicules.

Besides, he has dandruff.

↳ **In more, he has films.**

Boris est gros, mais il ne fait pas le poids.

Boris is fat, I grant you, but he doesn't pull his own weight.

↳ **Boris is fat but he doesn't make the weight.**

◆ ◆ ◆

Il est toujours fichu comme l'as de pique.

He's always dressed like a scarecrow.

↳ **He's always knackered like the ace of spades.**

Il essaie de péter plus haut que son cul.

He thinks he's a bigger deal than he really is.

↳ **He tries to fart higher than his ass.**

◆ ◆ ◆

Il n'y va pas avec le dos de la cuillère.

He doesn't go in for half measures.

↳ **He doesn't go there with the back of the spoon.**

Il ne se sent plus pisser.

He's too big for his boots.

↳ **He doesn't smell himself piss.**

◆ ◆ ◆

Pour se faire mousser, il a tenté l'opération de la dernière chance.

He made a last-ditch attempt just for the sake of showing off.

↳ **In order to lather himself, he tried the operation of the last chance.**

Il a mis le paquet !

He went all out, didn't he?

↳ **He has put the parcel!**

Au 10 Downing Street, il paraît que c'est la zone.

They say that 10 Downing Street has become very inhospitable.

↳ **At 10 Downing Street, it seems that it is the zone.**

◆ ◆ ◆

BoJo va être Gros-Jean comme devant.

BoJo will soon be in a tough spot.

↳ **BoJo will be Big John like in front.**

Il a du plomb dans l'aile.

He's in a bad way.

↳ **He's got lead in the wing.**

◆ ◆ ◆

Il va bientôt se prendre un râteau.

He will soon get shot down.

↳ **He will soon take himself a rake.**

On va lui rentrer dans le chou.

We'll give him a hard time.

↳ **We'll get him in the cabbage.**

◆ ◆ ◆

Pauvre Mme May, elle était à côté de ses pompes.

Poor Mrs. May, she was away with the fairies.

↳ **Poor Mrs. May, she was on the side of her pomps.**

Et elle en a encore gros sur la patate.

She is still peeved.

↳ **She has still big on the potato.**

BREXIT

Le Brexit est arrivé sans crier gare.

Brexit came without warning.

↳ **The Brexit is arrived without shouting station.**

Le Brexit ? Des économies de bouts de chandelle.

Brexit? It's just a way to pinch pennies.

↳ **The Brexit? Savings of ends of candle.**

◆ ◆ ◆

Le Brexit ? Ça coûte la peau des fesses.

Brexit will cost a fortune.

↳ **The Brexit? It costs the skin of the buttocks.**

C'est de la confiture
pour les cochons !

It's nothing but pearls before swine!

↳ **It's jam for the pigs!**

◆ ◆ ◆

C'est pas un deal, c'est un bide !

It's not a deal, it's a flop!

↳ **It's not a deal, it's a belly!**

C'est pas le Brexit qui va faire bouillir la marmite.

Brexit won't bring home the bacon.

↳ **It's not the Brexit which will make boil the pot.**

◆ ◆ ◆

Le Brexit ? Une couille dans le potage européen.

Brexit is a big fly in Europe's ointment.

↳ **The Brexit? A ball in the European soup.**

Le Brexit ? C'est pas de la tarte.

Brexit is no picnic!

↳ **The Brexit? It's not pie!**

C'est du lard ou du cochon ?

It's neither fish, flesh nor fowl.

↳ **Is it bacon or pig?**

◆ ◆ ◆

Un vrai sac de nœuds.

A real can of worms.

↳ **A true bag of knots.**

De la bouillie pour chats.

A load of hogwash.

↳ **Porridge for cats.**

◆ ◆ ◆

Le Brexit ? Ça vous fait de belles jambes !

A fat lot of good Brexit will do you!

↳ **The Brexit? It makes you beautiful legs!**

Tout ça aux frais de la princesse !

All that at the taxpayer's expense!

↳ **All that at the cool of the princess!**

◆ ◆ ◆

Votre Brexit, on n'en fait pas tout un fromage.

That Brexit of yours, let's not make mountains out of molehills.

↳ **Your Brexit, we don't make all a cheese of it.**

En fait, il y a à boire et à manger, là-dedans.

It's a pretty mixed bag, in fact.

↳ **In fact, there is to drink and to eat in there.**

Ça ne va pas mettre du beurre dans les épinards.

It won't put butter on your bread.

↳ **It's not going to put butter in the spinach.**

◆ ◆ ◆

Le Brexit est déjà à l'article de la mort.

Brexit is already at death's door.

↳ **The Brexit is already at the article of the death.**

Je sens qu'il ne va pas faire long feu.

I have a feeling that it won't last long.

↳ **I smell that it won't make long fire.**

◆ ◆ ◆

Le ver est dans le fruit.

The rot has set in.

↳ **The worm is in the fruit.**

Et on s'en contrefout.

And we don't give a damn
about it.

↳ **And we counter-care of it.**

THE ROYALS

Faut pas pousser la reine
dans les orties !

Don't overdo it!

↳ **Don't push the Queen in the nettles!**

La reine n'est pas à prendre avec des pincettes.

The Queen is not in a good mood.

↳ **The Queen is not to be taken with tweezers.**

◆ ◆ ◆

La reine n'y a vu que du feu.

The Queen didn't see it coming.

↳ **The Queen saw only fire.**

On dit que la reine sucre les fraises.

They say the Queen is a bit doddery.

↳ **It says the Queen sugars the strawberries.**

◆ ◆ ◆

Il paraît qu'Elizabeth et Boris sont comme cul et chemise.

They say Elizabeth and Boris are hand in glove.

↳ **It appears that Elizabeth and Boris are like ass and shirt.**

Le prince Philip ? Il perd la boule.

Prince Philip? He's losing it.

↳ **Prince Philip. He loses the ball.**

◆ ◆ ◆

Il est à ramasser à la petite cuillère.

He's all washed-out.

↳ **He is to pick up with a coffee spoon.**

C'est un vieux de la vieille.

He's one of the old guard.

↳ **He's an old of the old.**

◆ ◆ ◆

Il est dur de la feuille.

He is hard of hearing.

↳ **He is hard of the leaf.**

Et les mauvaises langues disent
que c'est un vieux croûton.

And scandalmongers say
that he's an old geezer.

↳ **And bad tongues say that
he is an old crust.**

◆ ◆ ◆

Souhaitons qu'il ne casse pas sa pipe.

Let's hope he won't kick
the bucket.

↳ **Let's hope he won't break
his pipe.**

Le prince Charles pédale
dans la choucroute.

Prince Charles is floundering.

↳ **Prince Charles pedals in the sauerkraut.**

Camilla fait son âge.

Camilla does look her age.

↳ **Camilla makes her age.**

◆ ◆ ◆

Le prince Andrew est un propre-à-rien.

Prince Andrew is a good-for-nothing.

↳ **Prince Andrew is a clean-to-nothing.**

Il n'a pas inventé le fil à couper le beurre.

He's no Einstein.

↳ **He hasn't invented the thread to cut the butter.**

◆ ◆ ◆

Il vit aux crochets de sa mère.

He lives off his mother's back.

↳ **He lives at the hooks of his mother.**

Fergie n'a pas froid aux yeux.

Fergie is not faint-hearted.

↳ **Fergie hasn't cold at the eyes.**

◆ ◆ ◆

La princesse Anne aime mieux faire cavalier seul.

Princess Anne prefers flying solo.

↳ **The princess Anne likes better to make lonely horseman.**

C’est une bonne poire, William.

William is a bit of a sucker.

↳ **William is a good pear.**

Harry a été assez gonflé pour jeter un pavé dans la mare.

Harry had the nerve to set the cat among the pigeons.

↳ **Harry was enough inflated to throw a stone in the pond.**

◆ ◆ ◆

Il s'est barré, je crois qu'il a bien fait.

He cleared off, I think he made the right choice.

↳ **He crossed himself, I think he made well.**

Les petites-filles de la reine sont dans leurs petits souliers.

The Queen's granddaughters are feeling most uncomfortable.

↳ **The Queen's small daughters are in their small shoes.**

THE ENGLISH

Pauvre Shakespeare qui doit ronger son frein.

Poor Shakespeare must be chafing at the bit.

↳ **Poor Shakespeare, who must gnaw at his brake.**

Amis anglais, vous faites fausse route.

My dear English friends,
you are completely mistaken.

↳ **English friends, you make wrong road.**

◆ ◆ ◆

Tout nouveau, tout beau ? Pas sûr.

You say a new broom sweeps clean? I doubt it.

↳ **All new, all nice? Not sure.**

Et nous ? On compte pour du beurre ?

Don't tell us we count for nothing!

↳ **And us? We count for butter?**

◆ ◆ ◆

Nous ne serons pas votre vache à lait.

We won't be your cash cow.

↳ **We won't be your cow at milk.**

On a d'autres chats à fouetter.

We have other fish to fry.

↳ **We have other cats to whip.**

◆ ◆ ◆

Vous poussez le bouchon un peu loin !

You're going a bit far!

↳ **You're pushing the cork a bit far!**

Votre Premier ministre ment comme un arracheur de dents.

Your Prime Minister is a born liar.

↳ **Your Prime Minister lies like a teeth snatcher.**

C'est Boris qui fait son beurre, pas vous.

Boris is making his pile, you are not.

↳ **It's Boris who makes his butter, not you.**

◆ ◆ ◆

Vous avez les yeux plus gros que le ventre.

You're biting off more than you can chew.

↳ **You have the eyes bigger than the stomach.**

Vous allez y laisser des plumes.

You'll get your fingers burnt in this business.

↳ **You will leave feathers there.**

◆ ◆ ◆

Tout ça va bientôt tourner en eau de boudin.

All that will soon peter out.

↳ **All that will soon turn in water of black pudding.**

Vous allez vous en mordre les doigts, un de ces quatre matins.

You will soon be kicking yourselves.

↳ **You're going to bite you the fingers, one of these four mornings.**

◆ ◆ ◆

Il est encore temps de renverser la vapeur.

There's still time to reverse the trend.

↳ **It's still time to spill the steam.**

La Grande-Bretagne est maintenant sens dessus dessous.

Great Britain has been turned upside down.

↳ **Now Great Britain is sense on sense under.**

Je connais des Anglais qui rient jaune.

My English friends can't help giving a forced laugh.

↳ **I know some English who laugh yellow.**

◆◆◆

Ce n'est pas bien de faire des gorges chaudes sur les Macron.

It's not nice to poke fun at the Macrons.

↳ **It's not fair to make hot throats on the Macrons.**

Depuis le Brexit, les Anglais sont mi-figue, mi-raisin.

Since Brexit, the English have been half in earnest, half in jest.

↳ **Since the Brexit, the English are half-fig, half-grape.**

◆ ◆ ◆

Les Anglais ont le cafard à cause du Brexit.

The English have the blues because of Brexit.

↳ **The English have the cockroach because of the Brexit.**

Ils ont toujours tiré au cul.

They are real slackers.

↳ **They have always pulled at the ass.**

◆ ◆ ◆

Ils vont vite se crêper le chignon.

They will soon get into a catfight.

↳ **They will soon pancake themselves the bun.**

L'Angleterre et la perfide Albion, c'est kif-kif bourricot.

England or perfidious Albion – it's much of a muchness.

↳ **England and perfidious Albion, it's marijuana-marijuana donkey.**

L'économie anglaise ?
Bonjour les dégâts !

The UK economy is in a right shambles!

↳ **English economy?**
Good morning the damages!

◆ ◆ ◆

Vous avez lâché la proie pour l'ombre.

You chased rainbows.

↳ **You have left the prey**
for the shadow.

Tout ça n’est pas du tout cuit.

It’s no piece of cake.

↳ **All that is not all cooked.**

◆ ◆ ◆

Boris ne vous a pas fait une fleur.

Boris didn’t do you any favours.

↳ **Boris hasn’t made you a flower.**

Il vous a menés en bateau.

He took you for a ride.

↳ **He has led you in boat.**

◆ ◆ ◆

Et vous êtes tombés sur un bec.

And you hit a snag.

↳ **And you are fallen on a beak.**

Vous ne pouvez pas avoir le beurre et l’argent du beurre.

You can’t have your cake and eat it.

↳ **You can’t have the butter and the money of the butter.**

Vous pensiez vous faire des couilles en or ?

Did you think you'd be rolling in it?

↳ **You thought you would make yourselves golden balls?**

◆ ◆ ◆

Il ne faut pas prendre les vessies pour des lanternes !

Don't think the moon is made of green cheese!

↳ **Don't take bladders for lanterns!**

Vous avez du plomb dans l'aile.

You are in a sorry state.

↳ **You have lead in the wing.**

◆ ◆ ◆

C'est vous qui allez essuyer les plâtres.

You'll have to deal with the teething problems.

↳ **It's you who will wipe the plasters.**

Votre île est en train de prendre l'eau.

Your island is sinking.

↳ **Your island is taking the water.**

◆ ◆ ◆

Votre pays est au point mort.

Your country is at a standstill.

↳ **Your country is at the dead full stop.**

La fin du Royaume-Uni est cousue de fil blanc.

The end of the United Kingdom is utterly predictable.

↳ **The end of the United Kingdom is stitched with white thread.**

Les chiens aboient, la caravane passe.

Let the world say what it will.

↳ **The dogs bark, the caravan passes.**

◆◆◆

Le parti travailliste avale trop de couleuvres.

The Labour Party is swallowing too many insults.

↳ **The Labour Party gulps too many grass snakes.**

Les conservateurs ? Un panier de crabes.

The Conservatives are always at each other's throats.

↳ **The Conservatives? A basket of crabs.**

◆◆◆

Mais maintenant, ils ont le cul bordé de nouilles.

But they are very lucky now.

↳ **But now they have the ass bordered of noodles.**

C'est plus fort que de jouer au bouchon !

That's the limit!

↳ **It's stronger than to play at the cork!**

◆ ◆ ◆

C'est vraiment fort de café !

That's a bit steep!

↳ **It's really strong of coffee!**

C'est la goutte qui fait déborder le vase.

It's the straw that breaks the camel's back.

↳ **It's the drop that overfills the vase.**

Allez vous faire cuire un œuf !

Get lost!

↳ **Go make you cook an egg!**

◆ ◆ ◆

Vivre sans vous, c'est simple comme bonjour.

Living without you is as easy as pie.

↳ **To live without you, it's easy like good morning.**

Votre accord ne casse pas trois pattes à un canard.

That deal of yours isn't worth writing home about.

↳ **Your deal doesn't break three legs at a duck.**

◆ ◆ ◆

Vous avez filé à l'anglaise.

You took French leave.

↳ **You have spun at the English.**

Vous vous êtes jetés dans la gueule du loup.

You threw yourselves into the lion's den.

↳ **You are thrown yourselves in the wolf's mouth.**

◆ ◆ ◆

Revenir dans l'Europe ? Des clous !

Getting back into Europe? Not on your life!

↳ **To go back in Europe? Nails!**

Arrêtez de faire la fine bouche !

Stop turning up your nose!

↳ **Stop to make the fine mouth!**

Vous allez vous donner un mal de chien.

It will be a devil of a job.

↳ **You'll give you a harm of dog.**

◆ ◆ ◆

Arrêtez de faire des châteaux en Espagne !

Stop building castles in the air!

↳ **Stop to make castles in Spain!**

Ce n'est pas au vieux singe
qu'on apprend à faire la grimace.

You can't teach your grandmother
to suck eggs.

↳ **It's not at the old monkey that we teach to make faces.**

◆ ◆ ◆

Un tuyau : gardez une poire
pour la soif !

Let me give you a tip: just try
to save up for a rainy day!

↳ **A hose: keep a pear for the thirst!**

THE FUTURE

BoJo sera bientôt aux abois.

BoJo will soon be in dire straits.

↳ **BoJo will be soon at the barks.**

Qui ne perd rien pour attendre ?

Who will be in a lot of trouble?

↳ **Who doesn't lose anything to wait?**

◆ ◆ ◆

Boris va vous mener à la baguette.

Boris will have you under his thumb.

↳ **Boris will handle you at the stick.**

Vous allez faire un four.

It's going to be a complete flop.

↳ **You're going to make an oven.**

◆ ◆ ◆

Vous allez vite avoir la gueule de bois.

You'll soon have a nasty hangover.

↳ **You'll soon have the mouth of wood.**

Vous allez vous saigner à blanc.

You will bleed yourselves dry.

↳ **You're going to bleed at white.**

◆ ◆ ◆

Vous allez boire le bouillon.

You'll be in the soup.

↳ **You will drink the broth.**

Vous allez faire chou blanc.

You'll come up empty-handed.

↳ **You are going to make white cabbage.**

Vous allez rester le bec dans l'eau.

You'll be left high and dry.

↳ **You're going to stay the beak in the water.**

◆ ◆ ◆

Vous devrez vous serrer la ceinture.

You'll have to tighten your belts.

↳ **You will have to grip you the belt.**

Ce sera bientôt la fin des haricots.

The party will soon be over.

↳ **It'll soon be the end of the beans.**

◆ ◆ ◆

Boris va vous sucer jusqu'à la moelle.

Boris will bleed you dry.

↳ **Boris is going to suck you until the bone marrow.**

Tout ça va finir en queue de poisson.

It's going to fizzle out.

↳ **All this is going to finish in tail of fish.**

◆ ◆ ◆

Vous allez bientôt découvrir le pot aux roses.

You'll soon find out what's really going on.

↳ **You will soon discover the pot at the roses.**

Qui va payer les pots cassés ?

Who's going to pay the piper?

↳ **Who will pay the broken pots?**

On vous garde un chien
de notre chienne.

We will get even with you.

↳ **We keep you a dog of our bitch.**

◆ ◆ ◆

On se fiche de vous comme
de l'an 40.

We really don't care about you.

↳ **We don't care of you like of the year 40.**

Vous allez en baver des ronds de chapeau.

You'll have a hard time of it.

↳ **You will slaver rounds of hats.**

◆ ◆ ◆

Ne vendez pas la peau de l'ours avant de l'avoir tué.

Don't count your chickens before they've hatched.

↳ **Don't sell the skin of the bear before killing it.**

Importer du champagne ? Quand les poules auront des dents.

Import champagne? When pigs fly!

↳ **To import champagne? When the hens have teeth.**

◆ ◆ ◆

Et du bordeaux aussi ? Ce serait le pompon !

And claret too? That takes the cake!

↳ **And claret too? It would be the tassel!**

Boire du vin français ?
Vous pouvez vous brosser !

Keep drinking French wine?
You can go to hell!

↳ **To drink French wine?
You can brush yourselves!**

Et l'Irlande ? C'est une autre paire de manches.

As for Ireland, that's another story.

↳ **And Ireland? It's another pair of sleeves.**

◆ ◆ ◆

Mes amis, il faut sauver les meubles !

My dear friends, let's cut our losses!

↳ **My friends, we must save the furniture!**

À la bonne vôtre ! Et sans rancune !

Cheers! And no hard feelings!

↳ **At the good yours!**
And without grudge!

BORIS EN FRANCE

Boris au café

Je prendrai un ballon de rouge.

I'll have a glass of red wine.

↳ **I'll take a ball of red.**

J'aime faire cul-sec.

I like to drink it in one gulp.

↳ **I like to make dry-ass.**

◆ ◆ ◆

Un crème et deux allongés, s'il vous plaît !

One white coffee and two americanos, please!

↳ **One cream and two lyings, please!**

Je déteste le jus de chaussette.

I can't stand dishwater.

↳ **I hate the juice of socks.**

◆ ◆ ◆

Une blonde !

One lager, please!

↳ **A blonde!**

Et trois demis !

And three half pints of beer!

↳ **And three halves!**

BORIS AU RESTAURANT

Laissez-moi jeter un œil à la carte.

Let me have a look at the menu.

↳ **Leave me throw an eye at the map.**

On va prendre le haricot
de mouton…

We'll have some Irish stew...

↳ **We will take the bean of sheep…**

◆ ◆ ◆

… et des pommes de terre en robe des champs.

... and some jacket potatoes.

↳ **… and potatoes in dress of fields.**

Vous avez des coquilles Saint-Jacques ?

Do you have any scallops?

↳ **Do you have shells Holy Jack?**

◆ ◆ ◆

Et comme dessert on prendra deux chaussons aux pommes.

We'll have two apple turnovers for dessert.

↳ **And like dessert we will have a pair of apple slippers.**

BORIS AUX FOURNEAUX

Je fais revenir les oignons.

I brown the onions.

↳ **I make the onions come back.**

Et je fais sauter les pommes de terre.

And I sauté the potatoes.

↳ **And I make the potatoes jump.**

◆ ◆ ◆

Puis j'ajoute une noix de beurre.

Then I add a knob of butter.

↳ **Then I add a walnut of butter.**

Je cuis ma poule au bain-marie.

I cook the hen in a double boiler.

↳ **I cook my hen at the bath-Mary.**

◆ ◆ ◆

Et je la sers avec du gros sel
et un filet de citron.

And I serve it with cooking salt
and a dash of lemon.

↳ **And I serve it with big salt and a net of lemon.**

BORIS CHEZ LES FLICS

Vous allez être mis en garde à vue.

You will be placed in custody.

↳ **You will be put in keep at sight.**

On va vous tirer les vers du nez.

We will pry it out of you.

↳ **We'll pull you the worms out of the nose.**

◆ ◆ ◆

On va vous passer les menottes.

We're going to put the cuffs on you.

↳ **We're going to pass you the small hands.**

Vous serez traduit en justice.

You'll be taken to court.

↳ **You'll be translated in justice.**

◆ ◆ ◆

Et on vous mettra sous les verrous.

And we'll put you under lock and key.

↳ **And we'll put you under the bolts.**

Boris au volant

Appuie sur le champignon !

Step on it!

↳ **Press on the mushroom!**

Attention ! Tu viens de griller un feu !

Careful! You've just gone through a red light!

↳ **Careful! You come from grilling a fire!**

◆ ◆ ◆

Coupe le contact !

Turn off the ignition!

↳ **Cut the contact!**

Tu as un pneu à plat.

You’ve got a flat tyre.

↳ **You have a true at dish.**

◆ ◆ ◆

Défense de doubler !

No overtaking!

↳ **Defense to double!**

Boris chez le docteur

Je me sens tout chose.

I feel out of sorts.

↳ **I smell me all thing.**

J'ai tourné de l'œil.

I fainted.

↳ **I turned of the eye.**

◆ ◆ ◆

J'ai la tête qui tourne.

I feel giddy.

↳ **I have the head that turns.**

Je claque des dents.

My teeth are chattering.

↳ **I clack of the teeth.**

◆ ◆ ◆

J'ai une fièvre de cheval.

I've got a high fever.

↳ **I have a fever of horse.**

BORIS CHEZ LE COIFFEUR

On essaie une coupe en brosse ?

Shall we try a crew cut?

↳ **We try a cut in brush?**

Je vous coupe les pattes ?

Shall I cut your sideburns?

↳ **I cut you the legs?**

◆ ◆ ◆

Vous voulez des mèches rousses ?

Shall I put some ginger streaks in your hair?

↳ **Do you want some red wicks?**

Et une raie ?

What about a parting?

↳ **And a skate?**

◆ ◆ ◆

Non, faites-moi la boule à zéro !

No, shave it all off!

↳ **No, make me the ball at zero!**

Boris à la banque

Je voudrais retirer de l'argent.

I would like to withdraw some money.

↳ **I would like to pull again some money.**

En petites coupures.

In small bills.

↳ **In small cuts.**

◆ ◆ ◆

Je veux clôturer mon compte.

I want to close my bank account.

↳ **I want to put a fence around my count.**

J'ai signé des chèques en blanc.

I have signed a few blank cheques.

↳ **I have signed cheques in white.**

◆ ◆ ◆

J'ai un découvert.

I am overdrawn.

↳ **I have a discovered.**

Boris à la plage

Laisse-moi prendre un bain de soleil !

Let me sunbathe a moment!

↳ **Leave me take a bath of sun!**

Tu me passes de la crème
dans le dos ?

Will you apply suncream
on my back?

↳ **You pass me some custard
in the back?**

◆ ◆ ◆

Oh ! Un banc de sardines !

Oh! A shoal of sardines!

↳ **Oh! A bench of sardines!**

Oh ! Une étoile de mer !

Oh! A starfish!

↳ **Oh! A star of sea!**

◆ ◆ ◆

Oh ! Une baleine échouée !

Oh! A beached whale!

↳ **Oh! A whale failed!**

BORIS AU JARDIN

J'ai planté des choux de Bruxelles.

I planted some Brussels sprouts.

↳ **I have planted some cabbages of Brussels.**

Des petits pois.

Some peas.

↳ **Some small weights.**

◆ ◆ ◆

Et de la mâche.

And some lamb's lettuce.

↳ **And some chew.**

Il y a plein de mauvaises herbes.

There are a lot of weeds.

↳ **There are full of bad grasses.**

◆ ◆ ◆

Les groseilles à maquereau
sont mûres.

The gooseberries are fully ripe.

↳ **The currants at pimps
are ripe.**

BONUS

LE VOYAGE DE BORIS

Pour récompenser les lecteurs qui auront eu le courage de lire cet « énorme » ouvrage jusqu'au bout, nous avons pensé aux nostalgiques de ce bon vieux « franglais » de leur adolescence qui donnait des sueurs froides à leurs professeurs.

Nous avons donc imaginé Boris en voyage en France, en train de se régaler d'un « Bite-Mister » (croque-monsieur) après un spectacle aux « Madnesses Sheperdesses » (Folies Bergères). Son périple le mènera même jusqu'à Chin (Menton).

Eh oui ! Il fallait y penser…

Nous vous invitons d'ailleurs à considérer ce texte comme un jeu, sans oublier qu'il n'a évidemment, en aucun cas, l'imprimatur de l'Université.

Boris visite Paris

As soon as he arrived in Paris, Boris went to the Game of Palm and then he had a look at the Prison of the Health. Meanwhile his wife made heat up her blue card at The Good Market and at The Spring. Since it was lunchtime they went to the Street of The Look For Midday. After having a Bite-Mister, they took the underground at the Daughters of The Calvary and they stopped at Door Of The Lilac. Later, they went to the Father The Chair, and they took dinner near the Madnesses Shepherdesses. When they left, they had so bad at the feet that they couldn't wind up the Boulevard Good News. And it was much too late to go to the Sacred Heart.

Boris visite la France

Boris rented a Peugeot, he put himself on the line of right and got ready for the adventure. After Noisy-the-Dry he went to Azay-the-Curtain and then to the town of Towers. He drove to the Tray of One Thousand Cows where he expected his children to count the cattle in French. But the cows were nowhere to be seen. They went to The Well, where they took a dish of lenses. Since Saint-Stephen wasn't too far, he took his family to the Stadium of the Green… He made himself have by his kids who begged him to buy them green scarves and green wigs that they would never wear. The Mediterranean was calling, and the end South to The Big Lump. Italy was still a long way. They stopped their expedition at Chin.